בס"ד

Turtle
SUKKOT

by Jennifer Tzivia MacLeod

What's a turtle to do on Sukkot?
After Rosh Hashanah,
after Yom Kippur;
after a busy year.

Sometimes you just want to stay inside.

But Sukkot is a time to come out of hiding.

A time to welcome friends and family.

A time to share.

A time to dance.

And at Sukkot, the sky is vast and open.

The moon is high.

The world is wide awake.
The weather cools.
The rains begin.

Leaves fall from trees all around.

Next to the sea, young turtles must leave the place they feel most safe and snug.

Out in the world,
on our own,
we're vulnerable.
It's not always safe.

It's not always easy.

But we know Hashem is always watching.

Sometimes, a little company can be nice,

Waves of song rippling through the night.

What's a turtle to do on Sukkot?
It's not always easy to come out of your
shell.

To do something different.

To hatch, to move out, to move on.

But on Sukkot, with green all around,

We're in our natural element at last.

Right where we're supposed to be.

Chag Sameach!

חַג שָׂמֵחַ!

Happy Holidays!

About the Turtles

All the turtles in this book are green sea turtles, known by the scientific name *Chelonia mydas*. Here are a few awesome Chelonia facts:

- Unlike land turtles, sea turtles can't pull their heads into their shells.
- Sea turtles' front legs are shaped like flippers and don't work well on land.
- *Chelonia mydas* can grow very big—the largest ever found was 5 feet (152 cm) long and weighed 871 pounds (395 kg)!
- They live along the coasts of over 140 countries, all over the world.
- *Chelonia mydas* sea turtles can live for 70 years or more.
- Females become adults and can lay eggs when they are 25 to 35 years old.
- Young *Chelonia mydas* eat some insects and other sea animals, but adults are the only completely vegetarian sea turtles.
- The hard shell, or carapace, of *Chelonia mydas* can include dark brown, green, yellow, and black. They are called "green" sea turtles because of a layer of fat underneath that is green from their plant- and algae-based diet.

Of course, turtles don't really celebrate Sukkot—a festival for Jewish humans! But there *are* some important lessons turtles can teach us about Sukkot:

- *Chelonia mydas* usually prefer to be alone, but sometimes there is safety and strength in numbers. At Sukkot, we celebrate outside our comfortable homes and synagogues, so we usually also share it with friends and family.
- Sea turtles need healthy water to survive. Ancient rabbis compared the Torah to water. We can be better, stronger Jews if we build healthy connections to Torah and to mitzvot like the sukkah, lulav, and etrog.
- Sea turtles face threats all over the world: pollution, habitat loss, and climate change. The Jewish people have often faced threats, too. The sukkah symbolizes the way that Hashem has protected us through it all.

The Jewish Nature Series:

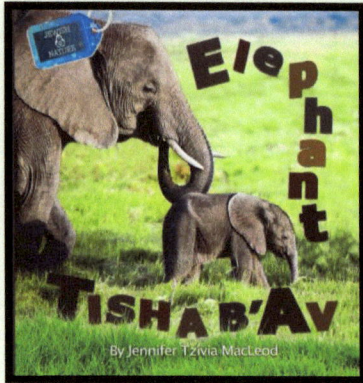

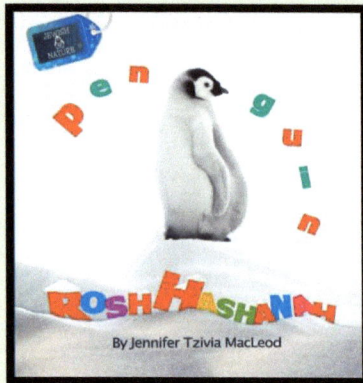

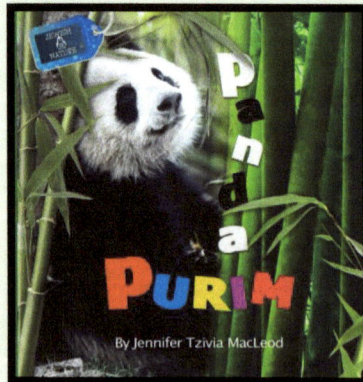

Penguin Rosh Hashanah

Caterpillar Yom Kippur

Turtle Sukkot

Owl Hanukkah

Panda Purim

Otter Passover

Elephant Tisha b'Av

Discover them all at:
http://tinyurl.com/JewishNature

About the Author:

Jennifer Tzivia MacLeod is a proud mother and grandmother living in northern Israel with her family. A freelance writer for magazines and newspapers, she also loves writing stories for Jewish families everywhere.

Can you help me out?

As an independent children's writer, I count on readers like you to leave feedback for others about my books. If you and your kids liked this book, please take a minute to leave a review:

http://tinyurl.com/TurtleSukkot

Thanks! ☺

www.ingramcontent.com/pod-product-compliance
Lightning Source LLC
Chambersburg PA
CBHW041551040426
42447CB00002B/136